First published 1985 by
Walker Books Ltd
184-192 Drummond Street
London NW1 3HP

Text © 1985 David Lloyd
Illustrations © 1985 Peter Cross

First printed 1985
Printed and bound by L.E.G.O., Vicenza, Italy

British Library Cataloguing in Publication Data
Lloyd, David, *1945* –
Breakfast. – (Dinosaur days)
I. Title   II. Cross, Peter   III. Series
823'.914[J] PZ7

ISBN 0-7445-0297-7

BREAKFAST

Written by David Lloyd
Illustrated by Peter Cross

WALKER BOOKS
LONDON

So-So-Slowly set out
for breakfast.

trump

trump

trump

Little So-and-So
rode on her
back.

bump

bump

bump

Little So-and-So fell off.

He ran about.

hooph

He fell into
a footprint.

They came
to the forest.

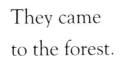

The leaves were
too high up for
Little So-and-So.

A leaf floated down, and another, then more and more.

Snip snap

One leaf flew away.

It was a butterfly.
Little So-and-So
chased it.
He never saw
all the creatures
in the forest.

But they saw him.
They followed him.

Rotter

Softy

Lazybones

Jelly Bug

Sneak

Slowcoach

Show-off

Dotty

Busybody

Pipsqueak

Creep

Fuzz-buzz

sssssSSSSS

SSSSSSTOPPPPPPPPPPPPPP!

Little So-and-So
stopped just like THAT!

CrumppPpPPPpPppPp

The creatures piled up
behind him.

There were butterflies
everywhere

everywhere

everywhere

everywhere

Snip snap

Little So-and-So
was off again.

hip hop

Close behind him
came Busybody
and Pipsqueak.

snip
snap
hip
hop
glup

Little So-and-So ran
right into the mouth
of a greedy glupper.

boing

The mouth banged shut.

Yeeeeeeeeeeeee

Busybody squealed

for help.

bzzz bzzz zip

All the creatures
flew at the glupper.

flop

The glupper's mouth
fell open.
Little So-and-So
tumbled
out.

In the forest
Little So-and-So
was playing with
his friends.
So-So-Slowly
reached down.

Goodbye, friends.
It's time to go.